Holding the Pencil

Encourage your child to hold the pencil properly. The child should hold the pencil gently in between the thumb and the forefinger, about 1 or 2 cm above the tip.

The pencil should rest on the middle finger for proper support. This gentle grip allows the child to move the pencil easily for smooth writing movements.

Left hand

This book will help you to observe which hand the child favors. If your child is left-handed, tilt the page at a clockwise angle so that the top left corner is slightly higher than the right. Place the paper slightly to the left of the child's body to prevent smudging of letters.

Right hand

Keep your hand relaxed.

Bend your fingers, not your arm.

Don't press the pen too hard.

Practice

The handwriting of your child will improve if you encourage them to practice their motor skills constantly. You can encourage them to write on the sand, color the alphabets or cut alphabets with safety scissors.

a

apple airplane acorn

Trace the Letter.

a a a a a

a a a a a

b

banana ball boat

Trace the Letter.

b b b b b

b b b b b

C

cup
cupcake
car

Trace the Letter.

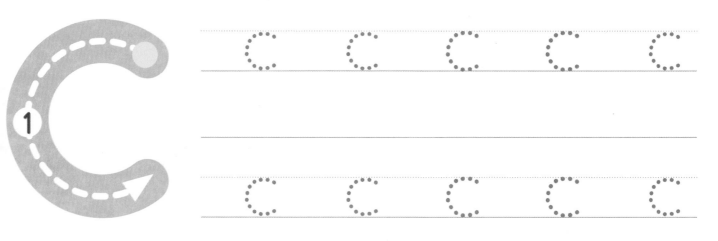

C C C C C

C C C C C

d

doll
doughnut
drum

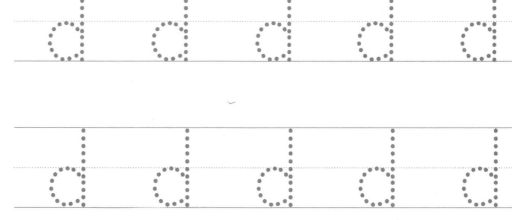

Trace the Letter.

d d d d d

d d d d d

e

egg

eye

earth

Trace the Letter.

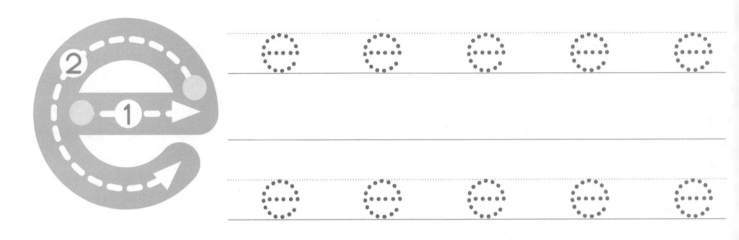

e e e e e

e e e e e

f

flower

french fries

fan

Trace the Letter.

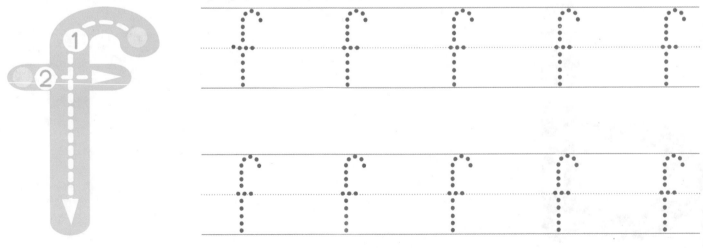

f f f f f

f f f f f

g

grape gift guitar

Trace the Letter.

g g g g g

g g g g g

h

honey helicopter house

Trace the Letter.

h h h h h

h h h h h

i

ice cream

island

igloo

Trace the Letter.

j

jug

jam

jacket

Trace the Letter.

k

kettle

kitten

kite

Trace the Letter.

k k k k k

k k k k k

l

lemon

lollipop

lamp

Trace the Letter.

m

mango   mitten

mask

Trace the Letter.

m m m m m

m m m m m

n

nest

nose

napkin

Trace the Letter.

n n n n n

n n n n n

o

orange   olive   onion

Trace the Letter.

O O O O O

O O O O O

p

puppet   peach   pizza

Trace the Letter.

p p p p p

p p p p p

q

queen   quilt   quail

Trace the Letter.

q   q   q   q   q

q   q   q   q   q

r

rocket   rainbow   robot

Trace the Letter.

r   r   r   r   r

r   r   r   r   r

S

ship

skate

sun

Trace the Letter.

S S S S S

S S S S S

t

tomato

truck

tent

Trace the Letter.

t t t t t

t t t t t

u

umbrella   utensil

unicorn

Trace the Letter.

U U U U U

U U U U U

V

van

violin

vase

Trace the Letter.

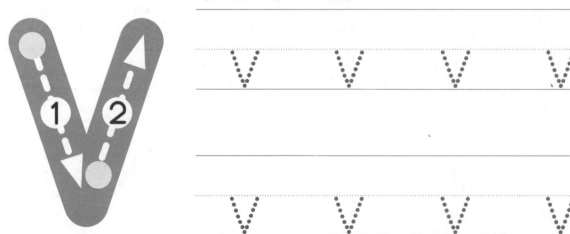

V V V V V

V V V V V

W

watermelon watch windmill

Trace the Letter.

W W W W W

W W W W W

X

x-ray fish x-ray xylophone

Trace the Letter.

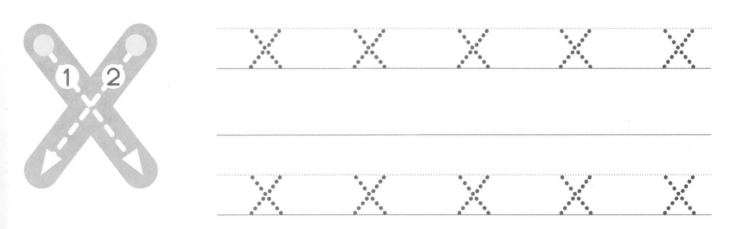

X X X X X

X X X X X

Y

yogurt   yarn   yacht

Trace the Letter.

Y Y Y Y Y

Y Y Y Y Y

Z

zucchini   zinnia   zip

Trace the Letter.

Z Z Z Z Z

Z Z Z Z Z

Draw a line along the abc path till z and help MAYA enjoy the sundae ice cream.

Write th_ Missing L_tters!

a _ _ _ e

_ _ h _

_ k _ _ n

_ _ _ r

_ _ u _ _

x _ _